Harry is miserable in her new house and won't be consoled. She had been so sure that Shipton would be by the sea. So imagine her delight when she catches sight of a boat drifting along the top of a green bank beyond the garden fence! She is thrilled to discover two horse-drawn narrow-boats, worked by two children of her own age!

The next minute she's helping out, as Ned the butty boy and his sister Bess make their long canal journey to deliver their cargo of coal to the paper mill. This is a journey Harry will never forget.

The Butty Boy is a wonderful evocation of canal life in the 1880s. Jill Paton Walsh has been fascinated by canals for many years, and at one time owned a narrow-boat cruiser.

Jill Paton Walsh studied at Oxford and was a teacher for three years before she took up writing. She has written nearly twenty books, mostly fiction for children, as well as short stories and numerous articles on writing and children's literature. As popular in America as she is in the UK, she is a winner of the Whitbread Award and the Boston Globe/Horn Book Award.

JILL PATON WALSH

THE BUTTY BOY

Illustrated by Juliette Palmer

Puffin Books

PUFFIN BOOKS

Published by the Penguin Group
27 Wrights Lane, London W8 5TZ, England
Viking Penguin Inc., 40 West 23rd Street, New York, New York 10010, USA
Penguin Books Australia Ltd, Ringwood, Victoria, Australia
Penguin Books Canada Ltd, 2801 John Street, Markham, Ontario, Canada L3R 1
Penguin Books (NZ) Ltd, 182–190 Wairau Road, Auckland 10, New Zealand

Penguin Books Ltd, Registered Offices: Harmondsworth, Middlesex, England

First published by Macmillan London Ltd 1975
Published in Puffin Books 1986
3 5 7 9 10 8 6 4

Copyright © Jill Paton Walsh, 1975
Illustrations copyright © Macmillan London Ltd, 1975
All rights reserved

Printed and bound in Great Britain by
Cox & Wyman Ltd, Reading
Typeset in Garamond

Except in the United States of America,
this book is sold subject to the condition
that it shall not, by way of trade or otherwise,
be lent, re-sold, hired out, or otherwise circulated
without the publisher's prior consent in any form of
binding or cover other than that in which it is
published and without a similar condition
including this condition being imposed
on the subsequent purchaser

For the navigators of the MARY BEATRICE

I would never have had the courage for it
myself. It was my cousin Harry who did it.
She was eleven when she did it, and I was
eleven when she told me about it; though by
that time she was nearly grown-up herself. I
was having a really dreadful time that summer,
staying with Cousin Harriet, and so dread-
fully, awfully bored I thought I could hear

my hair growing.

It wasn't exactly Harry's fault. The trouble was Edward. Edward was some family friend of Aunt Edith's—or rather the son of some friend of hers, and he was, we were told, madly suitable as someone for Harry to fall in love with and marry, and he liked her very much, so he had come to stay in Aunt Edith's big house in Warwickshire to see a lot of Harry, and try to win her affections. But Aunt Edith was ill—not what I'd call ill, with a fever and a furry tongue, and unable to eat even chocolate cake, but the sort of ill that meant she had to lie on a sofa under the open windows, sighing and reading every other page of a book—and so although she could "keep an eye on the young people", as she put it, when they were sitting on the other sofa, heads down over some puzzle or game, and giggling together, she couldn't walk out with them. And it seems the more people would like to be alone together when they are trying to win each other's affections, the less they may be, so someone is needed to follow them

around, just getting frightfully in the way—
and, yes, you've guessed it: the someone was
me.

Aunt Edith had borrowed me specially to
go walking with Harry and Edward, and
pointed out to my mother how good the
country air would be for me. And she did
give us scrumptious teas, and smile a lot, and
say, "Thank you, Kate," when she asked me
to do things, but I don't think anyone had
troubled to consider how *very* uncomfortable
it is to be sent running off all the time after
people who would much rather you were not
there.

We were all three walking on the canal
bank, when Harry first mentioned it, on our
way to find a good place for a picnic. It was
Harry who had suggested the canal. Edward
had looked dubious, and mentioned Shooters
Wood, but now we were here he said, "I say,
Harriet, what a topping place!" I thought it
was rather good, too, especially the little
bridge made of rosy red brick, with a parapet
of stone, and a cast iron plate saying *"47"* on

it, at which we had left the lane and climbed down onto the towpath. The bridge tapered a little towards the water, so that its reflection made a figure of eight when you looked back at it from the towpath.

It was a very prickly, uncomfortable sort of afternoon, in spite of us both liking Harry's canal so much, and, just for once, it was not because Edward and Harry were talking together all the time and taking no notice of me. And it was not because the only notice they were taking of me was to try to find ways to get rid of me, like, "Go and see if there are mushrooms in that field, Kate," or, "Oh, Kate, I've forgotten my shawl; just run back to the house and get it for me, will you?" No, Harry was paying me plenty of attention that day, pointing out flowers and butterflies beside the path, and it was "Look Kate!" instead of "Look, Edward!" for the dragonfly, and the heron, though he did get the kingfisher pointed out to him. But somehow they were a bit cross with each other, though not in the least admitting it, and the prickly feeling made me feel uncomfortable, too.

When we came to the next little bridge, we crossed by it into the hayfield on the opposite bank from the towpath, for Harry said we mustn't sit on the towpath or we'd be frightfully in the way. While we lingered on the bridge, dawdling in the heat and looking into the green water, some boats came by. First we saw a horse on the towpath, plodding towards us. It had its nose in a brightly-painted tin of oats, and a tiny girl in a scruffy overall trotted beside it, leading it, and holding on by a string of coloured wooden beads which the horse wore, Harry said, to stop the harness rubbing. Behind the horse stretched the towrope, and at the end of the towrope the black prow of a narrow-boat came nosing round the corner, and, behind that, a second one.

"The butty boat," said Harry. "And beautifully van-dyked."

"*Van-dyked!* It's painted like a tea-tray!" said Edward, laughing.

"Nevertheless," said Harry, "that's what they call it."

The boats were laden deep into the water, so that the names on their front ends were almost washed by the gentle ripple they ploughed on the glassy surface. At the front of each boat was a painted board, decorated with bunches of roses and a castle standing by a winding waterway; down the centre of the boats were rows of stout posts, painted like harlequins with gaudy triangles, and along the posts a line of planks was laid, and green sideclothes were held almost over the cargo by ropes laced over and over these boards. At the back of the leading boat was a tiny cabin, with a cluster of children sitting on the roof, and a bronzed dark-haired working man, leaning on a huge upswept red and yellow tiller, stood at the cabin door, thrusting the tiller sideways to bring his boat round the bend.

The tiny child leading the horse squinted up at us, against the sunlight, and said, "Mornin'," from underneath the brown handkerchief she wore on her head.

We watched them cast off the rope and glide smoothly under the bridge before hitching up the horse again the other side. When the first boat was through, it pulled its butty boat through behind it, and the butty boat was being steered by a tough-looking girl in a white cotton apron, very brown and dirty, with bare head and bare feet, who looked sharply away from meeting our eyes, and did

not answer when Edward bade her good
morning.

"I ran away on one of those once," said
Harry.

"Oh, tell me another, Harriet!" said
Edward, grinning.

"True, quite true," said Harry. "Mother
said I wasn't to tell you about it on any
account, for it makes me seem such a vaga-

bond; but I think I *shall* tell you all the same, for you might as well know what I'm really like."

"I do know what you're like," said Edward, vastly amused. "You're not the sort to run off with a barge man!"

"It wasn't a Number One I ran off with," said Harry, plucking a stem of grass and smiling slightly. "It was his butty boy. Come on, let's take the basket and rug into the shade of that big tree, and I'll tell you about it."

So we spread out the cloth in the mown hay in the shade, and set out on it all the good things that Aunt Edith's cook had prepared for us, and while we ate Harry told us about the dreadful thing she had once done.

Harry said the trouble with her was, she got bored too easily. (How like me, *I* thought!)

She hated being a girl, expected to mind very much what she put on each morning, even though there was never anywhere to go. She had a very strict dull governess to teach her all her lessons, so she didn't even go out to go to school.

And then, when she was eleven, her father announced that the family was going to move. He didn't say where, or when, just that they were going quite soon, and he hoped that Harry would be particularly good because her mother and all the servants would have quite enough to do without having to trouble themselves about her.

Being good, Harry said, meant keeping right out of the way, and asking no questions. Even Susan, her nursery-maid, who was always gentle and kind with her, was too busy to talk, and the governess took no interest in her, but simply set Harry page after page of sums to do all by herself, while she wrapped up every piece of china in the whole house in newspaper, and packed things one by one into tea-chests.

Harry just sat over her sums, and day-dreamed. She thought of the thrill of living in a new place, of all the new things and faces that moving would bring. And most of all she dreamed of a house with a view from the windows, from the schoolroom window especially, and from her own bedroom, so that even when she wasn't allowed out, which was often, she could look out at least. And the view she dreamed of was of the sea, the wide blue sea. It wasn't entirely moonshine either, Harry told us ruefully; she had heard someone mention "near Shipton" as where they were going, and she thought Shipton would be a seaport.

So Harry pictured the sea for herself. She had never seen it. But in her father's study there was a big oil painting which showed the sea, covered all over with curly waves, and swarming with ships of all sorts and sizes, and bordered by wharves and quays with armies of swarthy men rolling barrels and heaving bales, so of course Harry thought the sea would be a splendid thing to have in view from a window—as good as a lantern show.

And then when they got to the new house, it was not by the sea at all, but in deep country.

It was a tall brick mansion, closed in on one side by a thick wood of tall trees, and with a dark dense hedge of holly screening it from the road. It had a garden, a stretch of green lawn, but even that was not open, but closed in by a steep green grass bank running just beyond the fence at the bottom of the garden, and entirely blocking out from view any prospect of fields or lanes or coppices beyond. Worst of all, Susan, although she had packed her things like all the other servants, and set out from the old house a day early, did not appear in the new house. The governess said that Harry was far too old to need a nursery-maid now, and Susan had gone to another family with young babies to need caring for.

Harry cried for three days, and told every-one, even her father, when he asked her how she liked her new home, that it was horrible, like a prison, and that made everyone cross with her, for they were all bustling round to make it nice, and her mother liked it a lot; it was just Aunt Edith's sort of thing— secluded, and peaceful and somewhat grand.

Harry spent most of her three days of weeping alone, locked in her bare new school-room, that had not even covering on the bare boards as yet, nor anything unpacked to sit on, but only a pile of boxes in the middle of the floor. On the third day she had stopped moping and crying, and so she was let down-stairs to take tea with her mother, and see the beautiful new drawing-room where the grown-ups were to have such serene good times together. Aunt Edith said if Harry was good and quiet, she could come down for drawing-room tea every day from now on; but the picture of the sea had been hung over the mantel shelf of the drawing-room fire, and Harry no sooner clapped eyes on it than she cried again, and so she was banished once more, and had to have her tea in the kitchen with Cook, who told her that it was very natural to be upset by all the goings on, and she, Cook, was upset too, and couldn't lay her hands on any pot, pan, or ladle when she wanted it, but that Harry and she would both find their way about, by and by.

Harry's father thought she looked pale and wan with all that crying upstairs, and so she was ordered out the next day, to play in the garden till lunch time, whether she liked it or not.

Harry didn't like it much. The garden seemed sunk in green walls of tree or grass, and almost full, at that early hour, of blocks of deep shadow. Harry looked resentfully at the tall green bank beyond the fence, and then she sat down on the wet grass, and, closing her eyes, she imagined the landscape beyond— full of roads and fields, and farms, and a wide, wide river going down to the shore, and, right at the back, a blue ocean, crowded with ships—steamers sporting their fluffy white smoke plumes, and lovely sailing ships. And when she opened her eyes again to scowl at the horrid green bank, there, along the top of it, a boat was moving by.

It was moving slowly and silently. Harry couldn't see the horse, or the towrope on the path the far side of the boat from where she sat, and it was a boat such as she had never seen before, or even imagined: like the ones we had just seen, long and black, and with beautiful painted posts in bright colours rising amidships. And when the back of the boat at last came into view from behind a willow tree, it had a little painted cabin, with a brass-bound black chimney, and a painted jug standing on the roof, and THOMAS JEBB CARRIER BRAUNSTON written on the side in handsome painted letters, with a brass-bound porthole in the middle. Harry could see a painted tiller, with a horse-tail plume flying bravely behind it, and, most astonishing of all, she could see, leaning on the tiller, a little boy in a tattered shirt and coloured braces, not much—no, *definitely* no older than Harry herself.

Harry was thunderstruck. How could a boat sail through the green grass and the stems of meadow-sweet? How? How possibly? She leapt up, and just before the

boat disappeared from view, she reached the
garden fence, and scrambled over it—it was
made of posts and rails like a farm gate, and
very easy to climb—and raced up the embank-
ment, slipping and sliding on the wet grass,
and clinging with hands as well as feet, and
gained the top.

The bank was brim-full of brown water,
and edged with flowers and reeds. It carried
the canal across a little fold in the land. On
the far side from Harry's garden was a towpath, and along the towpath a horse was
plodding, wearing—it seemed to Harry's
baffled gaze, for the horse was now some way
distant—a white lace cap like a grandmother,
and it was pulling not one boat, but two, of
which pair Harry had seen the second one
going by, and the second one did indeed have
at the tiller a small boy, with his face and
arms burnt brown by wind and sun.

"Hey!" cried Harry, staggering to her feet,
breathless at the top of her climb. "Hey,
stop!"

"Stop?" said the boy, turning very bright

blue eyes on her, and pushing his cap back from a mass of dark curls, to scratch his head in bafflement. "Can't stop, even I'd reason for to; and you ain't no reason."

"But I want to talk to you!" yelled Harry, stamping her foot. "I want to ask you . . . ."

The boat was steadily drawing away along the canal, and Harry's path was blocked a little way along by a thick hawthorn hedge.

"Tha mun cross over, then, and come along wi'," said the boy.

Looking round, Harry saw that a little brick bridge crossed over from the field beside the garden to the towpath, and she scampered back to cross by it quickly, and catch up with the boat again. It was covered thickly with cowpats let drop by the homeward cows from the pasture. Harry splashed through in her button boots, and stained her pinafore as she went. The long satin ribbons on her straw hat slipped loose, and the hat sailed off her head as she jumped off the stile between bridge and towpath. It landed on the water, and floated. The slight wash left by

the pair of boats moved it gently sideways till
it caught up in a wild-rose bush that overhung
the edge of the water. Harry spared it only
the briefest glance before deciding that she
couldn't reach it back; then she raced along

the towpath and caught her sleeve on a thorn, and the fine wool of her dress was ripped into a large hole on her arm.

The boat was moving away very smoothly and steadily, and, slow though its pace was,

she would have had trouble catching up with
it, had there not been a lock concealed just
round the bend, and that lock, moreover, full
when they needed it empty, so that horse and
boat and butty boat were all stopped. The
boat was called MARY and the second boat,
BEATRICE. Harry came up with them with a
stitch in her side, and breathless.

The boy was too busy to talk to her. And
Harry saw with astonishment that the leading
boat was being handled not by a real grown-
up, but by a big girl of about seventeen or so.
Harry watched them put cranked brass windlasses onto the winding gear beside the lock,
and, leaning and heaving, wind a great toothed
iron bar upwards, slowly out of the ground.
As they did so, the water at the foot of the
lock gate began to churn and boil like a pot
of Cook's good brown soup, and the water
in the lock began to fall away. A dark deep
cleft lined with slimy wet masonry opened in
the ground at Harry's feet. In the bottom of
it lay water, disturbed by a noisy white jet
escaping into it from a leak round the side of

the top gate.

The boy and girl waited patiently. Then they put their backsides against the great white balance-beam that reached across from the top of the lower lock gate and overhung the path beside it, and began to strain and heave backwards against it. It swung slowly away behind them, and the gate opened into a recess in the sides of the lock. There was a similar gate on the side of the lock on which Harry was standing, and while the others were scrambling across the catwalk over the top gates she put her own weight against her balance-beam, and walked backwards as they had done, and, greatly to her surprise, so massive and heavy did the whole contraption look, it moved smoothly and easily open.

The boy stopped half way across when he saw what she had done, and retreated, without so much as saying thank you. "Yah! Rosie!" he yelled at the horse, which leaned and started forwards, and he ran away down the path to jump aboard the leading boat, lift off the towrope that joined her to the butty, and

steer her in.

It didn't look to Harry as if the boat could possibly fit into the narrow slit at her feet, but it did—just—with an inch to spare either side, and the boy brought her in without touching. And it looked to Harry again as if the boat would not fit—as if it were far too long for the lower gate to close on it—but as the boy came, he flung an unwinding coil of rope to the girl, who caught it and dropped a loop of it over a bollard on the lockside, and tugged, and the boat came to a standstill just clear of the lower gates, with just an inch or so before her front end touched the upper ones.

Harry watched what would happen next, and as the girl closed one gate behind the boat, she swung on her balance-beam and closed the other one.

"Lower the paddle!" yelled the girl, tossing the brass windlass across at Harry.

"I beg your pardon?" said Harry, baffled, and not much liking being bossed around. But the girl had let the windlass on her side spin round a dozen turns, had taken it off the iron bar, and was running with it to the similar contraption at the other end of the lock.

"Let it run down, see," said the boy from deep below her. He looked up at her from his place at the tiller. "Lift that ratchet, and it'll go. Keep hold mind—or the windlass'll jump off and clobber you!"

Harry lifted the ratchet, and got her fingers covered in thick black grease. The oily bar dropped away rumbling into the ground, and the windlass ripped round and round, twisting in her grasp. When it stopped, she dropped the windlass, and nursed an aching wrist; saw her filthy fingers, and wiped them clean on her pinafore before she could stop herself.

"Go git the other one up, then," called the boy.

"Well, really!" said Harry crossly.

"Are ye helping or ain't ye?" said the boy, his bright blue eyes scowling up at her.

So Harry helped. Baffled at first, and not understanding the lock-gear, she wound the

paddles that filled and emptied locks, and
caught the rope, which was both wet and
grimy with coal dust, and several times got
wound round Harry herself as well as the
bollard it was meant for. Once, trying to
cross the lock to retrieve a windlass carelessly
left lying the wrong side, she tried to jump
down onto the roof of the cabin, and off
again, as she had seen the others do, and she
took a tumble through the top cloths, and
fell onto the cargo, which was coal.

She had never in her life worked so hard,
but the locks came quickly, one after the
other, every hundred yards or so, and each
had to have the boats worked through it one
at a time, and there just didn't seem to be
any time to stop and think. Perhaps two hours
later they had got both boats up through the
last lock in what the boy called "the flight",
though if that was flying, Harry muttered to
herself, she was sorry for birds. The boy
brought away the pair of windlasses from the
last gate, and they all sat down for a moment
on the cabin roof of the butty boat.

"Do you always have to work so hard?"
Harry asked them.

"Only when the bleeding lock-keeper's
having his bleeding lunch!" said the girl with
a sudden grin. Her face and lips were dark
with sunburn and coal dust, and her gums
looked amazingly pink and glossy when she
smiled. Harry was shocked at her swearing,
and thought how Susan, or her mother, would
blanch at such a word; at the same moment,
leaning over, she caught sight of her own
reflection in the glassy cloud-filled water.

She was dishevelled and filthy from top to
toe. It dawned on her that she would be in
terrible trouble for getting in such a state, if
indeed she wasn't already in terrible trouble
for running off out of the garden, and not
being there when they called her in, as they
surely might have by now—for the sun was
high and hot, and the dew was gone off the
thick grass and flowers of the path. And
Susan, who might well have hidden away her
dirty clothes, and washed and mended them
quietly, would not be there to run to.

Harry burst into tears.

"Wa's up wi' ye?" asked the boy. "Ast hurt your arm, winding them old paddles?"

"It's not that," wailed Harry, through her tears.

"That's easily done, that is," said the boy uneasily.

"What is the matter, then?" asked the girl. "For we maun be going onwards, and you'd best get back. And thank you kindly for aiding us along," she added after a pause.

Harry kept sobbing.

"Tell us, then," said the boy, gruffly.

Harry said she would get into terrible trouble when they saw how torn and dirty she had got her clothes. Indeed, her tears flowed freely as she thought of it, what with the disgrace she was in already for not liking the new house.

"Where are you from, then?" they asked her.

"The big house back there."

"And don' they treat you kindly?"

"No!" said Harry indignantly. "They don't!

I'm so homesick for the other house we've just moved from, and they take no notice of me at all, only to give me work to do, that I must do all by myself, for they're all too busy to help me, and I've spent the last three days locked in a bare room just for not being cheerful, and this morning they turned me out into the garden in the wet morning, and forbade me to come in!"

"It's a wicked shame!" said the girl with sudden passion. "They take childer into big houses, and then they don't find a mite of kindness for them, for all the work they get. Only beatings. Do ye ever get beaten, poor wench? For if ye do, ye'll get another for that torn sleeve."

"Oh, yes, I sometimes do," sobbed Harry. For her governess did use a ruler on her knuckles often enough, and the torn dress would surely mean worse trouble than adding up sums wrong.

"Mrs Wilkins at Spillers Lock needs a girl, Bess," said the boy, suddenly. "And she's a kind old body. Could we take the lass down to her along of us?"

"Oh, I dunno, Ned," said the girl. "She don't look much of a hand at things. Ma Wilkins wants a good worker."

"Can ye work hard?" asked Ned, looking hard at Harry.

"Certainly I can," said Harry haughtily, for she was filled with sudden relief at the thought of escape, of getting away from the horrid house, and not having to face up to the terrible scene for her spoiled clothes, and although somewhere in a sneaking way she knew that they would be worried about her, she really had no idea how much, and thought it would serve them right for being so harsh with her.

"They'll come after her," said Bess.

"A short way, mebbe," said Ned. "On the roads more like, sooner than herealong. What do they care? They'll just get themselves another girl from somewheres."

A slight twinge of fear troubled Harry, for she realised that she would in truth be searched after rather more keenly than the serving girl they had taken her for.

"We could do with a third pair of hands, indeed we could," said Bess. She again looked thoughtfully at Harry.

"Where's the harm?" said Ned.

"Stir theeself then, Ned, we'd best keep moving," said Bess suddenly.

"Gerrup, Rosie!" yelled Ned at the horse, twitching the towrope, and the horse shook her flanks, and leaned, and very slowly the boats began to glide forwards, and Ned leaned on the great upturned multicoloured tiller and swung the butty boat out into mid channel behind the main boat.

Harry sat in the sun on the cabin roof of the butty and chatted to Ned, watching Bess, in the boat ahead, steer with effortless skill against the sideways pull of the towrope towards the towpath bank. Bess wore a frilled white bonnet with a flounce hanging down to keep the sun off her neck, and Harry had not been mistaken, for the horse, Rosie, was wearing a bonnet too, of white crochet work. Ned said it was to keep the flies out of her ears.

Ned told Harry about Mrs Wilkins, a widow, whose husband had been the keeper of Spillers Lock, and how the Canal Company had let Mrs Wilkins stay on and take over her husband's duties, and how she needed someone willing and spry to help her open and close the gates and collect the toll money, and keep the kettle boiling for her cups of tea.

At length Ned let Harry try the tiller, with his hand on it beside her own while she got used to it, for you had to thrust it to the right to turn the boat's front leftwards, and left to swing right, like doing something in a mirror. The butty boat followed the course of the lead boat, and you had to steer clear down the middle of the canal—Ned called it "the cut"—and go round the outer side of any bend.

Harry was enchanted. She kept her eye fixed on the MARY, and felt the long length of the BEATRICE respond to her pressure on the tiller, slowly and smoothly. Ned instructed her on watching ahead. Along a straight reach, the butty boat was drawn smoothly along behind the lead boat, but on a bend the butty had to steer its own course, towards the outer bank, resisting the pull of the connecting rope as the lead boat turned.

Harry was learning nicely, until, as they came round a sharp corner, she suddenly saw coming towards Rosie on the towpath another horse, and behind it, remorselessly gliding towards them, the front of another pair of boats, going the other way.

"Oh, Ned!" she cried.

"Hold right, Harry, hold right," he said calmly, taking the tiller from her. Harry watched.

"They're unladen, so they pass over us," said Ned.

"Pass over?" said Harry, baffled. But the boy who was leading the horse coming towards them, led his horse between Rosie and the hedge, and as the two horses passed, pulled the bridle. His horse stopped for a mere moment, his towrope slackened, and he lifted it over Rosie's back. Then his horse tugged again, and the rope came rapidly across the MARY, high, because of the height of the towing posts.

To Harry's astonishment, the chimney on
the MARY's cabin bent before it, so the rope
swept on towards them. Ned, reaching up,
flipped a latch on their own chimney, bent it
double, ducked gracefully under the rope as
it passed him, and set the chimney up again.
He nodded to the man at the tiller of the other
pair. He hadn't taken his eyes off the curve of
the cut ahead of them, or stopped steering for
a moment.

Harry soon discovered why he was so easy
at it, for it happened again and again all
afternoon, as boats passed them working the
other way. Ned said there were just as many
boats going the same way as they, but they
would only see these when they were stopped
at a lock or tied up resting for they all moved
at much the same speed, and were spaced out
along the distance like beads on a string.

The sun baked down on them, and there
were birds and water-rats to look at, and
when they felt thirsty Ned fetched a brightly-
painted ladle covered in roses, which he

called "the dipper", and plunged it in the
painted jug which stood on the roof beside
the chimney, and the water came to their lips
warm and slightly tinny.

Once or twice they came to another lock,
and real work began again. The three of them
worked the boats and one side of the lock,
while the keeper worked the other. It was
much easier than the locks they had come
through without help at lunch time, but Bess
and Ned were very jumpy and nervous at
them just the same.

"What's the matter, Ned?" asked Harry,
wondering with a twitch of fear if perhaps he
was afraid that the lock-keeper would guess
she was a runaway, and start a hue and cry.

"Nowt," said Ned, glaring at her
ferociously.

By the late afternoon, Harry was very
tired. She could hardly lift her feet from the
ground, and became clumsy at jumping back
onto the boat as it left the locks. Twice she
put a foot in the water, nearly falling in. A
sort of inner clock inside her kept expecting

Susan or her governess to come and take her
home. But nobody came.

Bess brought out a painted nose-pan of
oats from the cabin of the lead boat, and
hung it on Rosie's bridle.

Harry wondered why she had not been
followed. The boats were not moving very
fast, and they could easily have been caught
up with. Obviously now Susan had gone,
nobody cared.

The day wore on into a long tranquil green
evening, and the boats still moved steadily
onwards. The water below them grew all
shiny with the low slope of the light; the air
became cooler and full of shadows. The sky
began to rainbow with watery sunset shades,
while a few streaky clouds high above them
still caught the sun, and shone silver, weaving
ribbons of brightness in the mirrored depths.
Clouds of insects hung over the water. Harry
got bitten.

At last, when it was nearly dark, they came
to a lock with a cottage, and a pub and
stables beside it, and here they tied up for the

night. The horse was unharnessed, and groomed, Ned brushing the lower parts, legs and flanks, which he could reach from the ground, and Bess, on a stool, dealing with the horse's back and shoulders. Rosie was an enormous shire horse, with great plumes of hair round her hooves which took Ned a while to comb out clean of burrs and mud-cakes, but he wouldn't let Harry help because Rosie didn't know her touch, and might get restive.

When Rosie was safely stalled for the night, Ned fetched a jug of brown ale from the inn and they retired for supper to the cabin of the MARY. The cabin on the butty was not being used this trip, Ned said, there being so few of them.

Inside, the cabin was like Harry's dolls' house, so small and neat and bright it was. Across the back was a wide bed over a cupboard, with lacy curtains hanging across it. Down the right hand side of the cabin ran a bench, which made a "side-bed" at night, and seating by day, and on the left side was a stove and cooking range, with a big brass rail round it to stop the kettle sliding off the hob, and rails over it to dry clothes on. A huge copper kettle shared the top of the stove with a black iron stew pot.

Between the stove and the bed stood a cupboard, with a prettily-painted door shaped like a church window and hinged at the bottom so that the door let down to make a little table when they sat to eat, and inside the cupboard was food. There was bread and cheese, and a clutch of moorhen's eggs that Ned had picked up that morning, and a copper caddy of tea. Spoons and forks lived in a little drawer below the table-top door, and below that was another little cupboard. Even the step by which they came down from the deck outside was the coalbox in disguise.

Every inch of cabin wall was covered with lace-edged plates, threaded with ribbon like fairground prizes, or with straps and hooks for hanging odds and ends upon, and the only movable objects in the whole tight little place, apart from cooking vessels, were

a little painted stool, and the oil-lamp that
cast so warm a glow on all the sparkling brass
and copper.

Bess served them with soup from the iron
pot, and broke an egg into each steaming
bowlful. Ned broke hunks off the lump of

bread and they sat and ate from battered tin-
ware spoons, too hungry to speak a word till
the bowls were empty and scraped almost
clean.

"Is there more, Bess?" asked Ned.

Harry was glad he asked, for she wouldn't
have liked to herself.

"Soup, yes, bread no, or there'll be nowt
for morning," said Bess.

Harry began to drowse in the warmth, and
yawn and nod.

"Out wi' you, then, young Ned," said his
sister briskly.

"Not for long, Bess. I'm cold and spent."

"Sooner you go, sooner you can come
back," said Bess, shutting him out.

She poured water from the warm kettle into
a bowl, and offered it to Harry to wash.
Harry, who had hardly ever had to wash
herself without Susan to help her, and never
without a large basin of water and mounds of
clean soft towels, did her best, but it was not
good enough for Bess, who took over and
scrubbed Harry's neck and arms and hands

with a flannel rag, till Harry glowed, and then began on herself with equal vigour. Harry noticed with a twinge of shame that Bess, though she had probably never had more than a pint of water a day to wash in, and had spent the day since Harry met her in just the same way as she, had not got nearly so dirty as Harry. Just the same, when she had removed all but her underwear, and taken off her flounced bonnet, and cleaned her face, she looked much younger, so that Harry, who had taken her for nearly grown-up—for quite a young woman—was startled, and suddenly more afraid.

"How old are you, Bess?" she asked.

"Fourteen, far as I know," said Bess.

"Aren't you too young to manage a boat on your own?" said Harry.

"Yes, daresay I am. Wouldn't be allowed on a Company boat, not till the skipper's twenty-one. I never done it before, and won't be let again in a hurry, even we do get down in time."

Harry would have gone on asking, but at

that point Bess had finished washing. She poured clean water for Ned, and laid out a towel for him; then she came and lay down on the bed with Harry, drew the curtains across, and, reaching up, knocked smartly on the cabin roof. Ned came in from the cold outside, and Harry could hear him splashing his bowl of water, and then emptying the slops outside.

When he had finished they drew the bed-curtain again, and Harry saw him lying on the side bench, with his jacket rolled up under his head for a pillow.

She felt suddenly terribly crowded and at the same time alone. She longed for her wide soft bed in the empty nursery of the old familiar house, and she felt like pushing Bess off the bed, or lashing out at the brown sharp-eyed strange faces so oppressively near her. Nothing had ever been allowed to happen to Harry; she had never been allowed out of sight for long, never allowed to run or climb in case she hurt herself, kept from being frightened, kept from being uncomfortable, always fetched home by bedtime. She simply couldn't believe this could be happening— were they *really* not going to find her, not going to come and take her home, and scold her, and put her safely to sleep in a wide soft bed by herself?

She choked back a sob, and turned over to face the wooden wall, shuddering to think of all that great weight of coal the other side of a few planks, only inches from her nose, and pretended to fall asleep. In a little while Bess put out the lamp.

The boat was not quite still. Harry couldn't *feel* it rocking, on the smooth water, but it somehow seemed softly afloat—not quite solid. And it wasn't quite quiet either; there were odd creakings, and faint watery noises from outside, and little tappings on the hull and the splash of a water-rat venturing out.

Harry was very warm now, under the crochet cover and close against Bess, and she ached a good deal from working so hard. Tiredness weighed down on her like a great load within her head, but she was so unused

to the murmurings and shiftings going on
around her that she couldn't quite sleep at
once, and so, by and by, she heard Ned
saying in a soft, urgent voice:

"Shall we make it, Bess, d'ye think?"

"I dunno, Ned, truly. But we mebbe shall."

"We've another pair of hands to the locks
now."

"And did we do right, I wonder?"

"We could do with the help, Bess. How'd
we have gone along so well today, if we hadn't
have found her?"

"That's right enough," said Bess.

"Well, so. We'm in the lurch, and we gotta
find help. And Ma Wilkins could do with a
girl."

"I'd be easier if she weren't so pretty-
spoken, or if she seemed used to showing
herself handy. If she'd noticed when the fire
needed mending, or summat. And Ned, when
we were washing, I saw not a mark on her."

"You fret too much, Bess," said Ned. "Why
would she come along wi' us except she
weren't happy?"

And Harry lay there, listening, really very frightened, and vowing to be handier at mending the fire and such like, and to take care to seem like a servant girl. For if it would have been bad enough to go back dirty at lunch time, it would be terrible— Harry couldn't even begin to imagine how bad—to go back after spending the whole night away, and so, clearly, she would just have to be a serving girl now, and work for Mrs Wilkins. The only trouble was, Harry had never taken the least notice of the servants except for Susan.

Still, she managed better the next day. It got easier as she got used to it. The boats could only travel each day as far as Rosie could manage; the horse was considered first in every way. They filled Rosie's painted nose-pan, gave her water, checked her hooves for stones every few miles, groomed her, made sure her harness did not chafe, cherished her in every way possible. Harry was awestruck at the sight of Ned's small form, bent over, holding across his crooked knees the enormous hooves of Rosie, with their flowing plumes of hair, looking for stones between shoe and hoof. Rosie took it calmly enough, though she had a tendency to start to lean against Ned. "Gerroff!" he would yell at her, just before she pushed him into the cut.

When they came to a lock it was the custom for the boat crew to work one side, while the lock-keeper worked the other, and Harry soon got used to playing her part in this. But between locks she could sit on the butty cabin roof, one hand on the tiller, watching England winding slowly by, full of pleasant sights; fields and churches, and raw new railway cuttings, and streams and farmhouses.

More often she would trot alongside Rosie, urging her on, and chatting to her, and seeing the wild flowers thickly clustered by the water's edge, many of them unknown to her as she had never been allowed in marshy places before. As she went she spotted moorhens' nests in the reeds, or startled rabbits, but she quickly learned not to tell Ned about the nests because he stole the eggs at once for their supper, and, oddly, Harry felt painfully sorry for the mother birds, returning to their empty homes. He found enough without her, anyway.

Sometimes she helped Bess on the lead boat, putting coal on the fire, and various things in the stew pot towards supper. Some of the things that went into that pot were lifted from canalside fields or gardens, and once there was a rabbit Ned hit with his catapult, and several times there were fish from lines Ned set in the evening. Ned was the first boy Harry had ever spent much time with, for the children invited to play with her at home had always been other little girls. She thought he was splendid, with his stocky toughness, and his cleverness at catching things, and his bright cheerful eyes.

When they passed a little shop on the tow-path they would spend a few pence on provisions, but even with Harry's pocket money that had been in her apron pocket, by good luck, there was very little to spend. Turnip broth was all they ate on more than one occasion. Just the same, Harry looked forward enormously to supper. She began to think food was really one of the very best things in the world; she had never in her life before been hungry enough to enjoy it.

Polishing brassware in the cabin and shining the plates was girls' work, but it was Ned's job to clean the brass bands on the chimney pots, and swab down the painted cabins, and the boats' names, MARY and BEATRICE on the front ends.

Harry soon learned to call the canal, "the cut", the reaches between one lock and the next, "pounds", and herself, casual worker as she was, a "huffler". She learned, too, the serious side of things and some of the meaning of the conversation she had heard between Ned and Bess on that first night. The Jebb

family had a contract with a paper mill to
bring down coal from the mines; Ned and
Bess's father was a "Number One" which
meant he owned his own boats, and worked
as his own master, supplying the paper mill.
MARY and BEATRICE were a pair he had bought
for his eldest son, Tom, to start up with.

"Tom's been waiting four year for a contract with the mill," Ned told Harry. "There's
always more Number Ones wanting work
than the mill owner can do wi', so he keeps a
list of men with good boats ready. And Tom's
name no sooner come to the top, than he
broke his arm, back up at the mine, loading
his first cargo; and we maun get his coal
down to the mill, or they'll give his contract
to the next man on their list. And he'll be in
trouble if we'm late with it, too, that's why
we'm pressed and fretful about the time we're
making."

"Rosie's a good horse," said Bess. "She'll
go on mile after mile with just the odd crack
of the whip from the boats to keep her at it.
But we go much faster and safer when she's

led along."

"It was lucky both ways we met you," said Ned.

"Please, Ned," Harry said, "I know I'm not used to any of this, but I'll do my best to help you more, if you'll just tell me how."

"You do well enough, for a lass, Harry," Ned said, quietly. "You got the hang of the tiller quicker'n what I did, that was born in a butty."

They all had enough to worry about, in fact. Harry knew there must be a search for her going on; Bess and Ned had Tom's cargo-date on their minds; all three were jumpy lest someone should notice that they were three children handling a pair of boats without an adult. But many of the other boats they passed had families on board, and children at the tillers or leading the horses, so that just the sight of children working the boats caused no remark.

At one lock, though, the lock-keeper was talking to a Canal Company Inspector as they worked through.

"Where's your Number One?" they asked Harry, as the water lowered her past their feet into the lock chamber.

"Down below, getting some sleep," said Harry unflinchingly. "We were working late yesterday."

"Did you hear that, Bess?" said Ned admiringly, as soon as they drew out of earshot. "That was dead artful, Harry. And you never even blinked. Good on you!"

Bess said darkly, "Yes, Ned, I heard her. She lies as fast as a dog can lick a dish, don't she?"

But, even then, their worries seemed very dreamlike and unreal to Harry. They couldn't exactly hurry; they went as fast as Rosie could pull, and could go no faster. And time simply wore away in a kind of hard-working tranquillity.

Just now and then Harry was overcome with attacks of homesickness. Once Ned saw the look on her face, and asked her if she was thinking about the big house, and Harry said yes. And Ned took her hand, and said to her very softly and kindly, "You put all that far behind you, little Harry. The world's a wide place, and you need never see that house again, nor anyone from it evermore get sight or sound of you." And at that, of course, Harry felt worse, though she tried bravely to smile at him.

Then that night, when the cabin doors were closed and bolted, and the three of them were lying snugly in the dark, Harry couldn't help crying.

Ned didn't stir, but Bess, who was lying so close to Harry, woke up and said sleepily, "What's up wi' thee, then?"

"Oh, nothing, Bess," said Harry, choking as she tried to swallow her sobs. "I'm sorry I woke you."

"Don't you like it on the cut, maybe?" whispered Bess. "Is it too hard for you?"

"Oh, no," said Harry. "I love it. And you are so kind to me."

"You running off from a hard place, and you liking it with us, then," said Bess. "There oughtern't to be much to weep for."

"I'm missing Susan," said Harry, with her eyes brimming again. "She was always good to me, and we had little jokes and secrets together. If they hadn't sent Susan away, I don't think I would have run off. . . ."

"Who's Susan?" asked Bess.

"The nursery-maid."

"Ah. However bad things get, like can always stick by like," said Bess. "That's what my ma says."

Harry didn't really understand that, but she was already nearly asleep, on her damp pillow.

They had been going four long days when they met real trouble. All the morning they met no boats coming the other way, as Ned uneasily remarked more than once. Then they came round a long bend in the cut, leading to

the next lock, and found a long line of boats
tied up, and others jamming the mid-channel,
and men and horses thronging the towpath.
Some way ahead they could see the lock;
across it a pair of sheer-legs made of tree
trunks made a wigwam-shaped outline against
the sky.

"Oh, no!" said Ned between his teeth.

They steered in to the towpath, knocked
in their mooring pins, and tied up, the butty
abreast of the leading boat.

"Better run up there, and see what's wrong,
Ned," said Bess. "And we'll go below and
stay there. Someone's gonna see we're alone!"

The two girls cowered in the cabin, with
the doors shut. In a while Ned came back,
nearly crying. "Some bleeding cock-brains
have silled their butty, and broken her back
in the lock, while they were drinking in the
inn," he said.

"Oh gawd," said Bess.

"What's it mean? What's 'silled'?" asked
Harry.

"It's letting the back of the boat lie over the

ledge below the top gates, when the lock is draining out," said Ned. "The back of the boat gets left high and dry on the sill, while the rest goes on down with the water, and the weight of the cargo has bust the bleeding boat. There's men down in the lock, cutting it up, and them sheer-legs ready to lift it out. All day! All day it will take, Bess! And the whole place crawling with Canal Company men to look cutty-eyed at us!"

"Whatta we gonna do, Ned?" said Bess helplessly. And just at that moment there came a smart rap on the cabin side, and a man's voice calling.

Very slowly Bess rose, slid back the hatch, and stood up into view.

"Where's Tom Jebb, then, girl?" said the voice outside. "These are his boats, aren't they? Tell him look sharp and lively, and go give his name to the lock-keeper. There's one pair of boats shoved ahead of him already, and he'll lose his place, an' miss his turn if he ain't careful."

"Can't we just wait here, then?" asked

Bess, in a shaky voice.

"You'll wait a week if you do. There's been men fighting up there already about who's to be first through when it's clear, and the constable called out to part them. The lock-keeper is making a list of who come when, and that's the order we'll go through in. He better get along there quick. You just tell him. Why, what's up, girl, 'taint the end of the world!"

"You a friend of Tom's, mister?" said Bess.

"Couldn't really say that," said the voice outside. "I know 'im. I ain't his enemy."

"He broke his arm, see," said Bess. "He ain't here."

"Who's in charge, then?" said the voice.

"Me," said Bess. "You won't tell on us, mister, will ye?"

"You and who else?" said the man.

Bess opened the cabin door, and he looked inside.

"We gotta keep his contract date," said Ned. "It's his first run."

"Ah," said the stranger. He was a tough-looking blond man in his mid-forties. He wore a wide leather belt with a boatman's windlass in it. "You're in a spot, then, aren't you? Tell you what I'll do. I'll go put your name down. Or Tom's rather. Anyone else bothers you, you tell'em Tom's gone off for an hour or two. We'll be just ahead of you, so when we get through I'll send my big boy to work your pair past the lock; he looks grown man enough. But meanwhile, don't you stay shut in here. A closed-up boat will make people wonder; you sit on the cabin like you hadn't a care in the world. Right then?"

"Oh, *thank you*!" cried Harry. "You are kind!"

"Oh, Tom'll do summat for me, sometime, don't doubt," said the stranger, moving off.

So they emerged and sat in the sun. Just in front of them a butty was tied up, with a woman sitting in the cabin door, cradling a baby and humming to it. Little groups of men chatted together on the towpath.

Time wore on. Harry and Ned went twice

to look at the work in the lock. The broken boat had been sawn apart. A false stern was being fixed across the end of her hold, to float her away, and the sheer-legs were being used to lift out the cabin section.

A great press of people stood around watching. Ned and Harry felt uneasy in the crowd, so they didn't linger there, but returned to the boats. They were no longer at the back of the queue; more boats had come up behind them, and still more came, every half hour or so, till the towpath was crowded for a mile or so back from the lock. The boatmen came up along the towpath, asking what was amiss, and cursing when they heard.

Harry skipped lightly across the front and back ends, and along the narrow toehold of the gunwale all round the boats, playing catch with Ned, while Bess, sitting drowsing in the sun leaning against the cabin door, grunted in annoyance as they brushed past her. Light-footed and cocksure, Harry ran down the line of planks laid amidships over the coal, and suddenly slipped, and rolled down the

sloping sidecloths over the side into the water. She came up gasping, clutched at the smooth slippery sides of the MARY's hull, screamed, and went under again. When she surfaced a second time, a stout man was leaning out from the MARY, reaching a hand to her, and Ned, white-faced, was holding the boat's shaft, which he had hooked into her dress to pull her in by.

"Don't, Ned, you'll tear it!" she said, spluttering and choking.

"Vanity at death's door!" said the man, getting firm hold of Harry's hand. "Blooming women." And he pulled her out, and set her, dripping, on the cabin roof. "You want to be more careful, young scamp," he said. "You can drown in the cut as quick as in the ocean. Lucky I was near, that's what. You wouldn't be cavorting about on the boats like that if your Number One were in sight, I'll lay you."

At the mention of the non-existent Number One they must all have looked scared, for he went on, "You may well look woeful. Drowning's no joke. Just two days back we come past a spot where they were dragging the cut for a young lady. All they could find was her hat."

"Heavens, Harry!" exclaimed Bess. "You're shaking like you had a winter wetting. You come and get outer them wet clothes at once!"

As the afternoon wore on, Harry lay in the cabin, while her clothes dried out, hanging over the stove, and Ned wandered on the towpath, keeping an eye on the work at the lock.

"You might as well take a kip, Harry," said Bess. "We won't be to bed early tonight."

It was very hot and sleepy in the cabin, with the sun beating down on its roof and wooden side, and the fire crackling quietly in the stove. Harry put her head down, and drifted to sleep.

She was woken by a sound of shouting a little distance off. The lock had been cleared, and the crowd were cheering. "Git your clothes on, then," said Bess. "We'll be moving shortly."

Harry put on her petticoats, very scratchy to her skin for they had dried stiff in the heat, and her woollen dress with the hole in the sleeve getting worse, and her pinafore. Her boots were hanging upside down over the kettle, and they, too, were stiff and hard to get on.

When at last she was laced and buttoned up, and she put her head out of the cabin hatch, she was surprised to see that it was nearly dusk. The trees cast long shadows, the sky was rosy pink behind the cornfield across the cut. The idle crowds on the towpath had become silent and busy; the horses were being harnessed up, the pins drawn, and the boats moved up towards the lock. Harry saw in the distance the lock gates open to reveal a pair of boats. They began to move down the cut towards her, their towrope passing over the roofs of the waiting line of boats.

It took a long time for the MARY and BEATRICE to reach the head of the queue. It was very nearly dark when they were suddenly joined by the big boy whose help they had been promised, and they worked through the lock at last. Above the lock many of the boats were tied up while the boatmen took their supper, and little discs of golden light shone from the lamplit cabins and were echoed in the dark water. The shadowy shapes of bushes overhung the towpath and cast everything into darkness, and there were voices in the gloom, and horses snorting and stamping while they were settled for the night. Bess and Ned took their boats up to the head of the moored line, and tied up there.

"I've only just got dressed," Harry complained. "And I'll have to undress again right away."

"Don't fear that," said Bess. "We'll stop and sup till the moon gets up, and then we go on. You'll have your clothes on a while yet."

"*Can* we move in the dark?" asked Harry,

astonished.

"Can if we must," said Ned. "Rosie done no work today, so she'll have some pull left in her. An' we maun git down to Mill Lock by today, or we'll not make Tom's date. Can you manage, Harry, do ye think?"

"*I'm* all right," said Harry stoutly. "I had a sleep this afternoon."

"We'm all right, likewise," he said. "'Twon't be the first time we've moon-lighted, nor the last."

So after supper the hatch was opened again, and they sat looking up at the square of black velvet pricked with stars that it left in the cabin roof, waiting for moonrise.

"We don't have any luck, when you come to think of it," said Bess, mournfully.

"Oh, I dunno so much," said Ned. "Could have happened at new moon, Bess, or in clouded weather. Or we could have missed meeting Harry."

When at last the moon was up and in sight over the sloping fields, the children climbed out into the air again.

"Shan't I bring the lamp?" asked Harry.

"No, no," said Ned. "It would blind us with brightness. We need to be owl-eyed. Just wait till your eyes open up to the gloom."

Ned was right. What seemed at first to be inky blackness outside, gradually took shape as a dark picture, like a very black woodcut in one of Harry's story-books. A pale frost of light lay over the silent land. The humps of hills, the treetops, the parapet of the next bridge over the cut, every upper side where a dusting of snow might lie in winter was frozen silver. A thin glaze of translucent sheen, like paper-thin ice, covered the surface of the canal. But every hollow, every lower growth, the bridge hole, the places where the hedge leaned over the towpath, or the sedges of the water's edge leaned over the water, were cast into a soft blackness as thick as nightmare. As the boats moved gently onwards, the surface of the water beneath them broke into dishes of pale light, rocking on an oily blackness, as globules of moonlight floated on the troubled surface. Behind them, when Harry looked back, the water was black, black, with only a dying line of moon-silvered wash trailing out behind them.

Yet they could see perfectly all they needed. They could steer down mid-channel as well as in daylight, except for one short stretch where trees leaned over the water on both sides, and threw a tunnel of moon-shadow across them. They passed a village with silver roofs, and a shining church spire, a ghost shine on the cobbled street beside the cut, and only one upper window lit, warm and gold. They passed a wide mile of farmland, with a ghost harvest on it, all of silver wheat, and a faint farmhouse where a dog barked crisp and clear across the silence. The locks were easy to see, their white-painted balance-beams showed clearly; but the lock chambers were so dark and deep, as the boats sank into them, that Harry almost cried with fright, shudder-ing, and looking up at the stars for comfort, and sighing with relief as the gates were swung back, and ahead of her, again, she could see the moonshine route of the next pound.

The lock-keepers were very cheerful and friendly, though it was so late; Bess said they were paid extra for night-work. And so they went on and on.

By the time they reached the Mill Lock they were like ghosts themselves, in their ghost landscape. They had long since fallen silent from weariness, and moved slowly, with heavy limbs. They had white faces, with deep black shadowed eye-sockets, and shining hair.

Just before the moon went down, they tied up the boat, and tethered Rosie where she could crop the towpath grass, and lay down, unwashed and still dressed, in the cabin, to instant sleep.

It was noon the next day, when they were still rather tired and cross from losing so

much sleep, that Rosie cast a shoe. Harry was
at the tiller of the butty when it happened,
and she had to bring it into the bank, and tie
it up before she could run up to join the other
two and see what had happened. They were
standing with stricken faces, talking urgently.
Ned was holding the worn shoe.

"We'll have to take Rosie on or back, and
then come back to the boats, Ned," Bess was
saying. "Either way we'll lose best part of a
day. It's ten mile back to the smithy at
Ponders Lock, and maybe even further to the
next one on. Face it, Ned," she said. "We're
not going to make it now. 'Tisn't our fault."

"It's mine!" cried Ned, almost weeping.
"I muster missed a worn nail when I checked
her hooves last night. But I did look, Bess,
honest I did!"

"What's wrong with the blacksmith back
there?" asked Harry.

"Back where?" asked Bess blankly.

"Just a quarter mile back, in the village we
just came through."

"There ain't no blacksmith there, Harry.

We'd know."

"He's new . . ." Harry began.

"We'd best get trudging back along," said Bess wearily. "I'm sorry, Ned, honest I am, but we just ain't going to make it. I never promised. I only said we'd try."

"But there *is* a blacksmith," said Harry, almost stamping. "Two hundred yards up the street from the bridge. *Newly established. All classes of work undertaken.* So don't worry, Ned; it's not far."

"Now, how would you know a thing like that, Harry?" said Bess, suddenly looking at her hard.

"There's a notice on the bridge, saying so, silly," said Harry, "in letters a yard high. Didn't you see it?"

But they both gaped at her. "Where did you learn to read, then?" said Bess, with a rather desperate note in her voice.

Harry realised too late that she had given herself away again. "Sunday School," she said bravely. "I used to go to Sunday School."

"I got enough on my mind," said Bess

miserably, "without fretting over who you are, or where you come from."

"There's a Sunday School in almost every village," said Harry hopefully, as though defending her fib.

"*I* wouldn't mind knowing how to read," said Ned. "Comes in handy, times like now. Come on then, let's get the old hoss to the smith."

And indeed there was a blacksmith, just where Harry said one would be, and he put a new set of shoes on Rosie within the hour, for eighteen pence, which Bess paid him out of a little oilskin bag from a drawer in the cabin ceiling which she called the monkey-box. And while they waited, the blacksmith's wife gave them a little round apple pasty each, hot from the oven.

On the fifth day, the canal went through a town. First, very close beside the cut, was a foundry—a great tall building with a towering black chimney from which smoke poured and lay across the sky like a thundercloud. Within the upper windows of this building fire could be seen, and on the desolate ground outside it, heaps of coal were piled. A narrow boat, tied up at its wharf, was being unloaded by three men with shovels. A smell of acrid and sulphurous air hung round them, and a racket of roaring flame and grinding machinery came from the blackened walls beyond.

Harry shuddered at this place, but Ned told her she would be hard put to it to get by without using iron. "Nails and stoves and saucepans, Harry, wheels and hammers and windlass gear, flat-irons and horseshoes, and coal-hole covers, and pipes and boilers and buckets and chains; there's folks labouring making iron for all of that, Harry, working all their lives in that building, not just roving past it!"

Beyond the foundry, the canal bank began

to be lined either side, at a little distance, by
street-ends of mean, close-packed houses, and
yards and sheds and wharves. The water in
the cut was black and opaque, slickened with
a treacly foulness. But the countryside came
with them in an ever-narrowing column,
infiltrating beside the water: a slender band
of grasses and valiant flowers, a little long

acre of waste land, like neglected meadow, in the heart of the stony town.

Great warehouses of sore red brick, grimed with soot, towered over the canal banks, and soon closed in on them from either side, till Rosie trod a narrow ledge at the foot of a cliff of hideous wall, and the boats swam behind her in a dark deep cleft, under a mere ribbon of distant sky, on water that lay in shadow from dawn to dusk.

At length the sinister wall to the right and the sinister wall to the left closed right round the canal like a clenched fist; they met and the canal disappeared into a dark hole under a blackened arch beneath. For a few moments Harry could see nothing in the gloom, and then she could just make out a pair of lock gates embedded in the darkness in the bowels of the black building. As they entered it, a band of dirty grey light crossed the boats; they came under not only the building, but the wide low arch of a bridge into the lock. Not more than a foot of daylight fell between tunnel and bridge arch. It was a deep lock, maybe twelve or fourteen feet of slimy blackened lock-wall dripping above them as they lay in the bottom of it. Then Ned raised the paddles, and the water began to boil and roll under them, raising them up out of the ground slowly and steadily and as lightly as though both boats and all their cargo were a pair of leaves floating.

Up they came, past the wet masonry of the
lock, and into the sweet sun and air again,
and found themselves in the middle of a
handsome town, with green public gardens,
and a fine tall church with a spire, and wide
streets thronging with people. The bridge
from under which they had come, carried the
London road on its way, loud with rolling
carriage wheels, and the terrible buildings
were chopped down to half height from this
higher level, and masked by a row of shops
standing in front of them. And from there
the canal bent away leftwards, past handsome
houses with gardens, and in hardly any time
at all it was out in the grassy fields again,
bringing with it, still, its trailing ribbon of
grassy bank, that had threaded the town
through from side to side. Ribbons, Ned said,
and gloves and carpets were what those town-
folk made for their livelihoods, for the most
part. Ned seemed to know a lot about such
things.

And after the dark town, as the afternoon
wore on, Ned and Bess became brighter and

brighter, and laughed and called to each other
and to Harry very merrily as they went about
their tasks, or stood at the tillers, and with
each lock they worked through, they became
lighter-hearted and more chirpy than before,
till Bess was almost skipping and dancing at
Rosie's side, and Harry guessed—of course—
that they were nearly at the paper mill, and
the burden that had gone off her companions,
like cloud-shadow off the countryside, was
the fear of missing Tom's contract. As for
herself, her own secret troubles seemed heavier
than ever, but she tried to smile back at Ned.

At last when it grew dark they tied up
beside a little cottage inn, and Bess set a
supperpot on the fire, and said, "Let's have
tune, Ned, while it heats through." And Ned
went down on his knees, and brought out
from the chest under the side-bed a little
painted thing like a pair of wooden platters
with a bellows between, from which he
squeezed a merry tune, with a fair-ground
sort of sound to it. Harry was entranced, and
the little accordion brought a group of other

boatmen out upon the lawn beside the inn with their beer-mugs in their hands who joined in the singing in a pleasant fashion and repaid Ned by buying the children a jug of ale to wash their dinner down. Harry didn't know any of the songs they sang, which were all about commerce and the arts, and toys made in Birmingham, and the Duke of Bridge-water. But Bess turned out to have a sweet and pretty voice, that Harry liked to listen to.

And so they slept like birds in the nest that night, curled up happily in the little cabin, and did not move till an hour after daylight, and, even so, reached the paper mill by eleven the next morning, and found the Jebb parents, with their own pair of boats, waiting there for them.

Ned and Bess brought the MARY and the BEATRICE expertly up alongside HOPE and FRIENDSHIP, two fine boats, nicely van-dyked, with w. JEBB *and Sons,* OWNERS *Canal Coal Hauliers* in swaggered letters on their cabin sides. A rosy-faced plump woman, her head enveloped in an enormous frilly bonnet, came

bobbing up through the cabin hatch on
FRIENDSHIP and said, "Hullo, loves," to Ned,
and, "Where's Tom then?"

There followed the most tremendous hulla-
balloo. A trio of smaller Jebb children, whose
very existence had not yet been mentioned to
Harry, crawled all over the cabin roofs,
attacking Bess and Ned with enormous hugs,
and mock punches, and shouting joyfully;
Bess began upon the tale of Tom's broken
arm, whereupon Mrs Jebb plied her with
questions about how bad he was in pain, and
Mr Jebb with questions about how long he
would be laid up, likely, and the uproar and
talking went on and on, only half understood
by Harry, who stayed nearby out of sight in
the cabin door of MARY, saying nothing. At
last, "So who did he get to bring his boats
down?" said Mr Jebb, looking around for
some non-existent person.

"He couldn't find nobody, Da," said Bess.
"Though he did try."

"The surgeon said he'd best stay up there,
where he could have an eye kept on him,"

said Ned.

"Didn't seem nothing for it, but to bring the load down on our own, Da," said Bess apologetically. "We done the best we could think of, so don' be angered."

"You'm telling me," said Mr Jebb, putting his enormous arms akimbo and leaning over his children from his six-foot height, "that you've come down from the colliery by your-selven, and no trouble on the way?"

"We did have a spot of help," said Ned. "We got a huffler along, sort of."

". . . a servant girl, Da," said Bess. "Running off from a harsh position, and we thought Ma Wilkins might take her, for she's handy enough, and willing, and pretty spoken."

"Let's have a look at you, then, little wench," said Mr Jebb, kindly enough, to Harry, who came slowly out of the cabin of MARY and stood trembling and shy before him. "Don't be afraid. We owe you something if you've helped my pair of scamps in doing so well for us," and he smiled at her, from eyes

as brightly blue as Ned's, so that she liked
him at once, in spite of his bristly chin and
rough clothes.

But Mrs Jebb said, "Mercy, Bess, that ain't
no serving girl! That's the child of gentlefolk!
What have you done, girl, what have you let
us in for!"

"She *said* she was a servant girl!" cried
Bess. "Go on, Harry, tell them—tell them
what you told us about being locked in and
locked out, and beaten!"

Harry blushed, and looked down, away
from the circle of accusing eyes.

"She can't tell us, for it ain't true," said
Mrs Jebb, grimly. "Look at her boots, Bess;
did you ever see a servant girl wear boots
like those? And look at the lace on her
pinafore. Oh, Bess, you oughter've known!"

"I wondered how come she could read,"
muttered Bess miserably.

"*Did* you tell my children that you were an
ill-used serving girl?" demanded Mr Jebb,
with real severity.

"Not . . . not exactly . . ." stammered Harry.

"I just let them think it, let them go on thinking it once they began to. I did say I had been locked out in the garden . . . and that was *true*! My father thought I looked pale . . . ."

"Well, you don't look pale now, girl," said Mrs Jebb. "Come, William, anyone could see she's come to no harm through us."

"It would be prison for taking a child, Ma," said Mr Jebb.

"We don't get copped if we just take her to Ma Wilkins," said Ned, hesitantly.

"Or leave her by the cutside somewhere lonely, and make off in a hurry," said one of the small children. Harry began to cry.

"We'll take her back where she come from," said Mrs Jebb. "That's all we can do. Now, stop crying, girl. We've got coal to unload, and our journeys to make. But we'll be past your house again within the month, and we'll put you off there. Maybe we won't get caught red-handed with you if we're careful."

"We'll take her back straight away, Ma," said Mr Jebb. "That's what we'll do. Tomorrow's Sunday, and I'm not starting to move my boats on Sunday, or half the folk on the cut will wonder what's up wi' me; but first thing Monday we'll go right back the way Tom's pair came down, and we'll have her home in three days or so, with luck."

"You'll miss the next week's cargo, going that way, William Jebb. And what will we eat, may I ask?"

"Bread and dripping for a week or two, I daresay," he said, frowning. "We've come through that before now, Ma."

"Even that will be hard to come by, with a whole cargo gone missing," said Mrs Jebb. "And we need a new towrope, bad, Will."

"I'll pawn me watch-chain," he said. "We'll eat that."

"And all for a flighty, selfish, lying child . . ." Mrs Jebb exclaimed. Ned's arm came suddenly round Harry's shoulders, and held her tight.

"Yes," said Mr Jebb, very firm and quiet. "Think of her family, Ma. What if it were one of ours? Rich folk have feelings same as anyone else." But he looked very severely at

Harry again. "*Did* you say you were beaten?"
he asked her.

Harry nodded through her tears. They were
tears of anger as much as anything. She had
never in her life before been called such
unkind things as Mrs Jebb had just called
her. "I get hit with a ruler when I get my sums
wrong," she said. "I do. It wasn't a lie. And
I'm *not* selfish either. How was I to know it
would get you into trouble? *They* should've
known! If it's so terrible, they jolly well
shouldn't have taken me!"

"Oh, Harry!" said Ned, taking his arm
from round her shoulder.

"You come with me, girl," said Mr Jebb
evenly. And he took Harry by the hand, and
led her off by herself, down the towpath to a
scruffy inn by the end of the wharves. Outside
the inn he called the pot-girl who was gather-
ing the dirty glasses from the tables in the
yard, and taking her by the other hand he
walked the two of them a little way further,
and through a farm gate into the corner of a
cornfield.

"Jessie," he said to the pot-girl, "I've a particular reason for asking what I'm asking you today, and it's worth a sixpence to me, and perhaps a kinder heart to this young lady. But I'd like you to show her what you showed my Bess the last time we was past here." And then he turned his back and looked at the corn. And the pot-girl lifted her dress up over her head, and showed Harry a thin bony back with red weals on it, and smudgy black bruises.

"*That's* what it is to be beaten, my girl," said Mr Jebb. And he gave Jessie a sixpence, and took Harry back to the boats without another word spoken.

After that it took the rest of the day for Mr Jebb and three or four other men to shovel the coal from MARY and BEATRICE out onto the paper mill wharf, and Harry was kept busy helping with the younger children, and peeling potatoes for supper.

The next day was Sunday, with bells ringing from a church not far away, and the Jebbs put on Sunday clothes, carefully unfolded from stowage chests under the side-beds in the cabins. Mr Jebb wore corduroy trousers, almost white with much scrubbing, and a wide belt and braces embroidered all over in a pattern of spider-webs in a dozen bright colours, and a shirt with a pattern of coloured triangles and lozenges on it, just the same as the pattern on the cratches on his boats. Over his shirt he wore a moleskin waistcoat with brass buttons and a velvet collar. Ned had clean shirt and trousers, and a spider-web belt, and a coloured kerchief at his neck; Mrs Jebb had a black satin dress, and a voluminous flower-sprigged bonnet, and a starched white apron, and Bess had a ruched and frilled dress of brown and white check, and a clean white bonnet, and there was something crisp and clean for the three younger ones too, but Harry, whose clothes were dirty and torn and who would not fit into anything of Bess's, had to be left behind in the boats. She sat alone and miserable, and polished some brassware in the cabin hoping to please Mrs Jebb.

Next day they turned the boats, in a

specially widened part of the canal that Ned
called a "winding-hole", and started to take
Harry home. The boats rode high out of the
water, unladen as they were, and went along
very smoothly and fast behind the horses,
but, even so, with two animals and four boats

to manage, there was a lot to do, and Harry couldn't help with it, because Mrs Jebb had taken all her clothes away, and she was wrapped in a blanket, sitting on a pile of roping and folded topclothes in the empty hold. Ned's small brother came and mocked her. "I hate you," he said. "We'll be hungry next week acos of you. And you look daft in that blanket."

But Ned said, "Don't worry, Harry, we've known worse. We was froze-in six weeks last winter, and down to our last hod of coal, and near starving afore the thaw. Bread and dripping in summer weather's nothing to that. *I* won't think hardly of you on account of that, honest!"

"Oh, Ned, I'm sorry though, I'm terribly sorry!" said Harry. "If only there was something I could do!"

As it turned out, there was something Harry could do. That evening after supper Mr Jebb opened a drawer in the cabin of FRIENDSHIP and brought out a Bible, very battered and tied together with ribbon. "I'm told you can read, young mistress," he said to Harry. "And it's seldom we get to hear from a book."

So Harry opened his Bible very carefully and they all squeezed into the little cabin, and listened and she read to them about Joseph and his brothers, and about David and Goliath, and about Noah's Ark. Then Ned said to her, "I wish I could write me name, Harry."

"I'll show you," she said, eagerly.

"Would you show me mine, Harry?" said Bess.

"And mine, and mine," chorused the children.

Mrs Jebb was sitting close by the lamp, mending something, but she raised her head, and told Ned where he might find a stump of pencil, and Ned brought a bundle of toll-tickets from the monkey-drawer to serve as paper. Harry wrote the names large and clear, each on the back of a ticket, and set her pupils to copy them below, over and over. They passed the pencil round from hand to hand in silence. In a while Mr Jebb pushed a blank

ticket across the little flap-table to Harry, and
said, "Would you show me mine, girl?"
Harry sat beside him, and guided his huge
hand on its shaky course round WILLIAM JEBB
over and over. And they worked at the
writing till bedtime.

The next evening the pencil and tickets
were brought out again, and again they set
to work.

"Do you want your name, Mrs Jebb?"
asked Harry, shyly.

"No, no, what use'd it be to me?" said Mrs
Jebb, shaking her head.

But the next morning, while Harry was
helping to dress the smallest child, Mrs Jebb
said, "What you could do, if you've a mind
to it, is read my plates for me."

So Harry read the plates that hung all round
the cabin of HOPE. *A present from Brighton*
said one. *God is not mocked* said another.
There was a shiny sugar-pink plate with a
picture of an iron bridge crossing from cliff
to cliff over a river, which said *Clifton Suspension Bridge,* and a jug with a picture of a little

girl sitting on a trunk in a fur-edged cape, which said *Somebody's Luggage,* and a china mug with pansies on it in relief, which said *Love the Giver*.

Mrs Jebb became more and more pleased, and found Harry more things to read, right down to *Hankey and Sons* on the cast iron stove, and *Made in Birmingham* on the brass coal scuttle.

On the last evening which Harry spent crammed into the little cabin with the Jebb family, Ned and Bess wrote so well, that she showed them how to write MARY and BEATRICE and HOPE and FRIENDSHIP as well as their names.

So the morning came when Harry woke to find the boats already moving, though it was dark still. As she wondered sleepily why, Ned came and shook her by the shoulder. "Wake up, Harry," he whispered. "Wake up. This is where we took you up from, and you've got to go!"

When Harry scrambled out onto the deck, Mr Jebb was waiting for her. He had his Bible laid on the open hatch. "You put your hand on that, and you swear to me, as you hope to live," he said to her, "that you'll not tell anyone—not anyone at all, not for any reason, my name, nor the name of my boats. You swear that, and you go safe home, and we go safe on our way."

Harry put her hand on the book and said, "I swear. Of course I won't tell," she added. "I wouldn't get you into trouble for anything, after you've been so kind to me."

"You think what you'm doing and saying, another time, girl," said Mr Jebb, smiling at her, "and fare you well now." And Ned said nothing, but pushed a folded toll-ticket into her hand. Then he said, "Gerrup, Rosie!" And the boats moved slowly away in the shadowy light of the very early morning, till they were out of sight among the dark willows on the canalside.

And so Harry came home again, appearing
in the garden one morning before anyone but
the kitchen-maid was awake, sun-tanned and
healthy, with her clothes immaculately clean,
and pressed, and the tears in them mended in
neat small stitches.

After the tremendous fuss had died down
a bit, Harry's family did try to make her say

whom she had been with. She would not. She told her father she had been with the boat people, but had sworn an oath not to name them. He told her very sternly what terrible grief and worry she had caused; how they had found her hat in the water, and dragged the cut for her dead body, and found no trace of her. And how her mother had been prostrate with shock and sorrow all the time Harry had been gone. He hoped she was very ashamed of herself.

Harry was, she was. And while she was apologising, with tears, for the grief she had caused at home, she let slip that she had also caused hunger and hardship to the folk she had been with, and then her father tried even harder to make her say whom they were, so that he could find them, and offer them money to repay them for their loss. But Harry felt quite sure that Mr Jebb would not be pleased by money that came from her broken word, so she still would not say, and her father could do nothing but thank God, and send a donation to an almshouse for retired boatmen run by the Canal Company.

"So there you are, Edward," said Harry. "That's what *I'm* like, and you might as well know it." She leaned over the picnic basket, and scooped the last of the potted shrimps onto her finger, and licked it slowly.

Edward grinned. "I assure you, dear Harry, that the manners of your rough companions have not in the least affected yours," he said.

"They weren't rough, Edward," said Harry sharply. "They were kind and gentle, and hardworking enough to deserve anyone's respect."

"Oh, *Harry*. Well, ignorant, then."

"Not that, either."

"You had to teach them to write their names, remember?"

"But look at what *I* didn't know. I didn't

know where and how iron was made, or
where the new railways went, or what sort
of lives people lived making the things I used
every day, like Ned knew; I hadn't seen the
rivers open out to the sea, or the great ships
loading from barges, or tunnels and factories,
and all those things. Compared to him, I
didn't know anything. But when I said that's
what I'm like, I meant it—I mean I'm the
sort who goes vagabonding. I mean to go to
all sorts of far-off places, and do all sorts of
wild things in my life."

"Wherever you want to go, Harriet," said
Edward, and he was looking at her very
fondly, with a kind of shine in his eyes, "I'll
take you."

"I don't want to be *taken,* Edward," said
Harry. "I want to be *let go.*"

He looked away at once. Then he said,
"Time to go home," and began to pick up
the picnic things.

We were sleepy with sunlight and full of
food, and we wandered slowly along the towpath, to the bridge that carried the lane up to

the house.

"Harry," I asked her, "can you remember any of the songs Ned sang?"

"Well," she said, "there was one that went:

Our commerce must thrive, and the arts soon
*   revive,*
Which are now in a sad situation,
If we follow this notion, from ocean to ocean,
To have a compleat navigation!

"And," she went on, "there was a very jolly one about, *The best of wrought metals is Birmingham ware!* and a very sad one about *Oh, poor old horse!*"

Edward roared with laughter.

"And there was a nice one about *Go where he will, he's my love still, my own dear navvy boy.*" Harry was humming it softly, but Edward was still laughing and did not hear her.

"But wasn't it good to be home, Harry?" he said at last. "Wasn't it spacious and cosy, and comfortable to be back again?"

"In a way. But I missed the cut too. It was still awfully dull at home most days, though they did send me on a day trip to the sea.

They brought Susan back somehow—I don't know what her new employers must have thought—and as soon as they could, they moved a mile, out of sight of the canal, where we are now. But, until we went, I used to sit in the garden watching the boats go by, and hoping and hoping to see MARY or BEATRICE again. But I never did."

"I don't blame them for moving," said Edward.

"Well, they couldn't stop me lying in the grass in summer, thinking about it," said Harry tossing her head. "Remembering the low light polishing the far end of the cut to green silver, and the trees hanging upside down on either side of a reach of mirrored sky."

"Think of it in winter," said Edward.

We reached the bridge, and climbed up to the lane. Just beyond the bridge, a pair of boats was tied up, waiting for the lock. A young woman stood at the tiller of one boat, and a handsome young man from another was sitting on the cabin roof, leaning towards

her, and chatting. He was wearing a velvet-
collared waistcoat like Mr Jebb's Sunday best,
and he had a red kerchief round his neck,
setting off his dark curls. Harry looked keenly
at him, pausing a moment before she turned

away. We left the canal behind us, and trudged home.

That night while we ate our supper in Harry's old schoolroom, I plucked up courage to ask her, "You're not going to marry Edward, Harry, are you?"

"No, Kate," she said, "I'm not. How did you know?"

"I just thought not," I said.

"Look, I'll show you something, Kate," she said. She went to her work box, and felt in the silk lining, and brought out a little folded piece of dark green card. TOLL *at* NAPTON TOP LOCK *one shilling a ton,* it said.

And on the back, in shaky large round writing:

HOPE and *FRIENDSHIP.*

Other Puffins by Jill Paton Walsh

A CHANCE CHILD

A powerful novel of a neglected boy's haunting journey along a canal, which takes him through time, from reality into fantasy.

THE DOLPHIN CROSSING

The story of two boys who took a boat to help save the stranded British army at Dunkirk.

FIREWEED

An unforgettable, poignant story of two teenagers adrift in London during the Blitz.

Some other Puffins

WILLIE THE SQUOWSE
Ted Allan

A funny, unusual tale of a very talented squowse called Willie, whose father was a squirrel and his mother a mouse. Illustrated by Quentin Blake.

THE COMPUTER NUT
Betsy Byars

When Kate receives a message on her computer from a mysterious admirer, she hopes it's her secret crush, Willie Lomax. But she eventually discovers – no thanks to 'help' from her best friend, Linda – that Willie is not the culprit. In fact, Willie turns out to be a resourceful computer sleuth when the two team up for hilarious close encounters with the alien comedian.

SHADES OF DARK
ed. Aidan Chambers

Eight original ghostly stories by distinguished authors known for their ability to conjure up strange images and exciting stories, including Helen Cresswell, John Gordon, Jan Mark and others.

DOLPHIN ISLAND
Arthur C. Clarke

Johnny Clifton had never been happy living with Aunt Martha and her family for the twelve years since his parents had died when he was four. So when an intercontinental hovership breaks down outside his house, he stows away on it.

THE WITCHES
Roald Dahl

No silly hats and broomsticks here! This is a book about 'real' witches – those that absolutely loathe children and are always plotting to get rid of them. A Whitbread Award winner.

CHARLIE LEWIS PLAYS FOR TIME
Gene Kemp

Cricklepit Combined school, which produced Tyke Tiler and endured Gowie Corby, is now coping with five of the numerous Moffat family. Trish and the others find they have a new teacher for their last term at Cricklepit, a strict disciplinarian who believes in silence, segregation and sex discrimination. But for one member of the family the worst thing is that Mr Carter has a passion for music.

THE BOYS WHO DISAPPEARED
Margaret Potter

David's mother is admitted to hospital early for the birth of her twins, and his stepfather is called away to perform an operation on a politician in India. What is to happen to David? In this exciting story of quest and discovery, two boys learn how to shape their own lives.

THE WAR OF THE BIRDS AND THE BEASTS
Arthur Ransome

As charming as Arthur Ransome's first collection, *Old Peter's Russian Tales*, though some of the more sombre tales reflect the dark side of the world of the Russian peasantry.

A PAIR OF DESERT-WELLIES
Sylvia Sherry

A vivid and enthralling story about a dare-devil gangleader who cheeks everyone and lives by his wits. (Sequel to *A Pair of Jesus-boots*.)

JELLYBEAN
Tessa Duder

A gentle, modern novel about Geraldine, or 'Jellybean', a young girl growing up in a one-parent family.

NICOBOBINUS
Terry Jones

Nicobobinus and his friend, Rosie, find themselves in all sorts of intriguing adventures when they set out to find the Land of the Dragons long ago, in Venice. Stunning illustrations by Michael Foreman.

FRYING AS USUAL
Joan Lingard

When Mr Francetti broke his leg it looked as if his fish restaurant would have to close, so Toni, Rosita and Paula decide to keep things going.